PUG PALS

TWO'S A CROWD

Flora Ahn

SCHOLASTIC INC.

ISBN 978-1-338-27713-5

10 9 8 7 6 5 4 3 2   18 19 20 21 22

Printed in the U.S.A.   23

First printing 2018

Book design by Mary Claire Cruz

One time my niece and nephew said to me, "Wouldn't it be cool if we opened your book and it was dedicated to us?"

For Dorothy and Theodore.

CHAPTER 1

Sunny couldn't place her paw on it,
but something felt strange.

But maybe that was just the grumbling in her empty stomach.

Sunny's human had forgotten to give her goodbye treats before leaving the house. Sunny's stomach growled loudly at the thought of the missing treats.

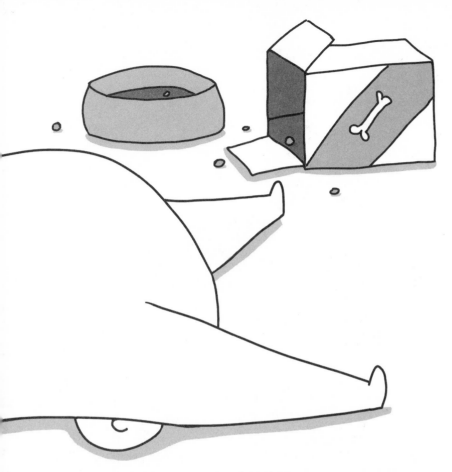

Sunny rolled down the couch and sought comfort in her usual routine.

First, she visited all the rooms, coated them with fur, and filled the air with her unique puggy scent.

Then Sunny found the brightest
sunbeam in the living room and
practiced her favorite yoga stretches,
from downward-facing pug to pawstand.

Lastly, she arranged her beloved stuffies
in order of size and inspected them.

She laid aside the ones that needed
some mending and moved
them close to the door.
That way her human would
trip over them right away
when she came home.

Sunny put the rest of her stuffies back into the toy bin and climbed on top of the couch. To take her mind off her rumbling stomach, Sunny counted down a list of her favorite things.

5. The moment bath time is officially over.

4. The rush of wind through her ears on a car ride (as long as it's not to the vet).

3. Watching a new episode of her favorite show, *Officer Bert: Paws on Crime.*

OFFICER BERT

PAWS ON CRIME

2. When her human comes home at the end of the day.

1. Her collection of stuffies— especially Mr. Bunny.

CHAPTER 2

Sunny didn't know it yet, but her world was about to be turned upside down in precisely thirty-two minutes. But for now, it was neighborhood surveillance time. After all, Officer Bert always said good neighbors should look out for one another.

A small movement down the street caught her attention.

False alarm. It was just her neighbors, Butter and Toki, approaching. Sunny eagerly jumped up to say hello.

But they walked by without a single woof or tail wag.

Sunny curled up and hid until they were
out of sight.

She rolled down the couch to find something that would cheer her up.

Sunny dug back through her toy bin and pulled out a slightly scruffy orange stuffie. She could always count on Mr. Bunny.

After turning in circles until she found the perfect comfy spot, she pulled Mr. Bunny close to her and settled in for a good chew on his arm.

Just as Sunny was starting to feel calm and drowsy, the sound of keys jangling against the front door startled her awake.

The door swung open,
revealing a shadowy beast.

Before Sunny could bark out in alarm, the beast charged straight at her and pounced.

Sunny dodged its sharp claws, jumped up and down, and growled. Those long hours watching Officer Bert had trained her for just this moment.

She would defend her home from this intruder!

The beast named Rosy
tore through the house,
leaving a trail of destruction
behind her.

Sunny waited for her
human to scold Rosy
and take her away.
But her human just
laughed and gave chase.

19

Surely, her human couldn't be serious!
Sunny closed her eyes.

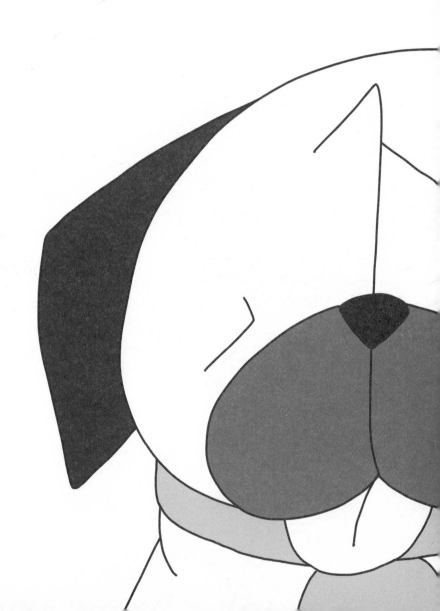

Her brief moment of peace was interrupted
by a strong puggy scent of corn chips and
a warm breath tickling her face.

Before Sunny could get a single word in, Rosy was already off skidding across the floor and knocking over Sunny's toy bin.

This all smelled wrong. Very wrong.

CHAPTER 3

The next morning, Sunny was disappointed to wake up and see that Rosy was still there. It hadn't all been a terrible nightmare as she'd hoped.

Everything continued to feel wrong that day. Normally, before her human did her daily disappearing act, she'd pat Sunny on the head and say, "You're the best dog in the whole world."

Today, she patted both Sunny and Rosy on their heads. "You two are the best dogs in the whole world."

Sunny noticed the difference.

Sunny's human turned to her. Sunny wagged her tail.

"I'm expecting you to take good care of Rosy while I'm away. She's family now."

Sunny's tail drooped. "She's not my family," she muttered.

After her human left and shut the door, Sunny shook Rosy off her drumstick. "Stop that!"

"I'm bored," Rosy said. "What are we going to do now?"

"I don't know what you're going to do," Sunny said, "but I have my usual routine to follow."

But Rosy made it a little harder
for Sunny to concentrate.

x

Finally, Sunny gave up. "Can't you go do whatever you want to do and stop bothering me?" she asked.

"STOP!"

"But I don't want to do something by myself," Rosy said. "I want to be with you!"

Remembering what her human had said, Sunny took a deep breath and tried to stay calm. "Fine. What is it that you want to do?"

Rosy's eyes lit up. She grabbed Sunny's paw and pulled Sunny behind her. "Yay! I have a great idea! We're going to have so much fun!"

But Sunny did not have any fun.

Nope.

Uh-uh.

Definitely
not.

The only actually fun thing was when Sunny turned on the television to watch *Officer Bert.* Rosy immediately stopped wriggling around and stared up at the big screen in rapture.

SUNNY'S TOP 5 LEAST FAVORITE THINGS ABOUT ROSY

5. Her frequent attacks on Sunny's drumsticks, ears, and jowls.

4. How she squeezed in to lick up any crumbs the second Sunny finished eating.

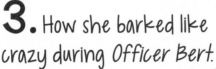

3. How she barked like crazy during *Officer Bert.*

2. The way she copied everything Sunny did.

1. How she stole and destroyed Sunny's beloved stuffies.

CHAPTER 4

Sunny curled up
on top of the
couch and double-
checked to make
sure that her
drumsticks were tucked in. If they
dangled over the side, Rosy might grab
them. This was the only spot in the house
where Sunny felt safe. Rosy was too little
to jump up. It had been thirteen days
since Rosy had arrived. Thirteen LONG days.

Rosy was the worst thing that had ever
happened to her. Rosy was the worst
thing in the entire world!

Sometimes when Rosy
was passed out from
her latest frenzy,
Sunny liked to close
her eyes and think
about the days when
she was the only
dog in the house.

She was doing just that when the couch
bounced and she felt the familiar and
unpleasant sensation of Rosy chewing on
her ear.

"Ha, I finally made it up here!" Rosy shouted in between slurps. "Ooh, everything looks different from up here!

"Does this window open? It does! Hey look, there are your friends, Butter and Toki. Hey, guys! Hellooooo!"

Butter and Toki looked up, but then quickly rushed down the street.

"Your friends aren't very nice," Rosy said. "How come they never want to play with us?"

"I never said they were my friends," Sunny growled, giving up on trying to ignore Rosy. "Can you be quiet for at least five minutes? And stop drooling all over my ear."

Rosy shrugged and dropped Sunny's ear from her mouth. "Fine. I'll just chew on . . .

Sunny watched Mr. Bunny's journey in horror.

"Look at what you did! I wish you weren't my sister!"

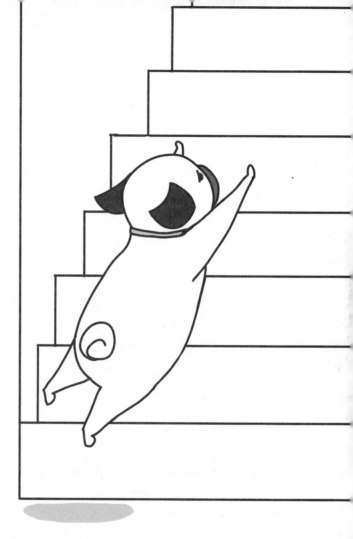

Sunny ran upstairs to have a good cry in her human's big bed.

CHAPTER 5

An hour later, Sunny's rumbly tummy demanded to be fed, and so she stomped downstairs.

She banged around the kitchen, slamming the cupboard doors and drawers as she climbed onto the counter to get some of her favorite cheesy crunchies to cheer herself up.

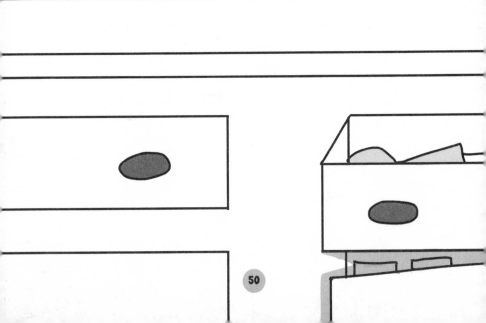

"I shouldn't have to hide upstairs," she grumbled to herself. "I was here first. I should get to stay in the living room with the cushions and toys. Rosy should go somewhere else."

Once Sunny finished her snack and cleaned up, she stormed into the living room. "I'm staying here, Rosy. I don't care where you go, but you can't stay in this room while I'm here."

Sunny blinked.
Rosy wasn't there.

A cool breeze fluttered through Sunny's floppy, black ears.

The one thing her human had asked her
to do was to take good care of Rosy. And
now Rosy was outside somewhere. Alone.

Rosy wouldn't know to avoid the big oak tree down the street where Mittens, the meanest cat in town, liked to lurk. She wouldn't know that Mrs. Carswell was very particular about her lawn and would run out yelling if any dog even tried to squat or lift a leg on it.

Sunny ran to the closet to get her gear. She had to go out and find Rosy before her human got back home.

"I can do this. I'm no different than Officer Bert, sniffing out someone's trail. Right?"

Sunny stepped outside and took three big sniffs. She followed the faint odor of Rosy's corn chips smell down the street.

As she passed by the neighboring houses, someone called out from behind a fence.

"Look who's finally out of the house by herself," Butter said.

"And off leash," Toki said. "Where could she be going? It's not like she has any friends to visit."

Sunny pulled her hood tight around her head to block out the sounds of their mean laughter.

Rosy was right. Butter and Toki weren't nice. And right now, Sunny didn't have time for their nonsense. Ignoring their taunts, she ran after Rosy's scent into the nearby park.

She didn't have to go very far before she heard a voice.

CHAPTER 6

"I'm sorry, I didn't mean to lose Mr. Bunny."

It was Rosy!

Hawks
Park

∗ Do not feed the hawks.

Before Sunny could call out, she heard a second voice, low and growly.

"It's all your fault. I'm the boss here and you have to do everything I say. So get out!"

Frowning, Sunny continued toward the voices.

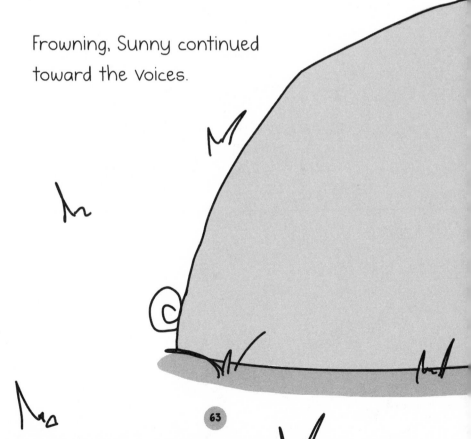

Rosy was sitting in front of a lumpy pile of rocks, mud, twigs, and leaves.

My belly and bottom aren't that big!
Sunny thought.

Sunny was about to storm in and yell,
but then Rosy hugged the fake Sunny.

"I said I was sorry," said Rosy. "I can fix
this. I promise."

Rosy hopped back and broke off one of fake Sunny's arms. "Excuse me, can I borrow this for a second?"

Rosy scratched some lines into the ground. "This is where we last saw Mr. Bunny, when he fell into a car. And Mittens said the car turned right at the end of the block."

Rosy sat back and rubbed her arm.

"Mittens was helpful, but he didn't have to get so mad and slap at me just because I wanted to see what his ears tasted like." Rosy made a face and shuddered. "They definitely were not as good as yours, Sunny."

Sunny felt so guilty watching Rosy playact with the fake Sunny. Rosy hadn't run away. She had gone off in search of Mr. Bunny.

Sunny hadn't been making it easy for Rosy, and she knew that the little pugling looked up to her. Sunny made some loud noises to announce her arrival.

Snort snort. Toot toot.

Rosy jumped up, knocking over the pile of rocks. "Who's there?"

"It's me, Sunny."

"You came looking for me?"

The little hopeful expression on Rosy's face made Sunny feel even worse about her treatment of Rosy the past few days.

Sunny pulled Rosy to her side. "Of course I came looking for you. You're my sister. Come on. I'll take us back home."

Rosy hesitated.
"I can't leave yet.
I haven't found Mr. Bunny."

"It's okay," Sunny said. "Forget about Mr. Bunny. What's most important is that I bring you back home."

"But I'm so close to finding him!" Rosy held up a small piece of orange fuzz. "See? A clue! He's close by. I know it! We can't just give up now. What would Officer Bert do?"

Sunny did want to get Mr. Bunny back. She'd already safely recovered Rosy, and they still had plenty of time before their human came back home.

She nodded. "Okay. Let's go find him."

CHAPTER 7

Rosy showed Sunny the spot where she had found the piece of orange fuzz.

"I couldn't figure out how to get in,"
Rosy said. "This fence goes on forever!"

Sunny carefully evaluated the situation.

Pulling off her backpack, she turned to Rosy.

"I think this looks like a job for Ninja Pug."

"Ninja Pug?" Rosy's eyes grew wide with excitement. "And maybe Ninja Pug's sidekick too?"

Sunny pulled out two dark suits and colored sashes. "Sure. And Ninja Pug's sidekick too. I always carry a backup suit just in case."

But even with their suits on, Sunny and Rosy had a little more difficulty with the fence than they had anticipated.

After a long struggle, they finally made it over the fence. Creeping and rolling across the grass, they stealthily approached a large building nearby.

They tried getting inside, but the door was locked.

"What do we do now?" Rosy asked.

Sunny thought about what Officer Bert would do in this situation.

Officer Bert, let's check the perimeter first for any open entry points.

Woof.

"Follow me," Sunny said.

Pressing her body against the building's side, she slowly rounded the corner.

"Now what?"

Sunny shushed Rosy and silently pointed up. Rosy nodded.

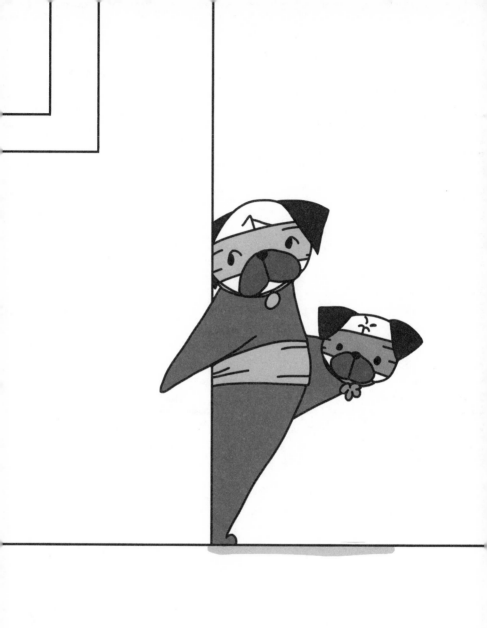

Pulling themselves up to the sill, they smooshed their noses against the glass and peeked through the window.

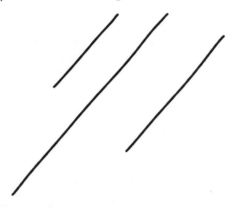

"Mr. Bunny!"

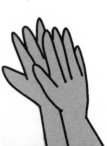

CHAPTER 8

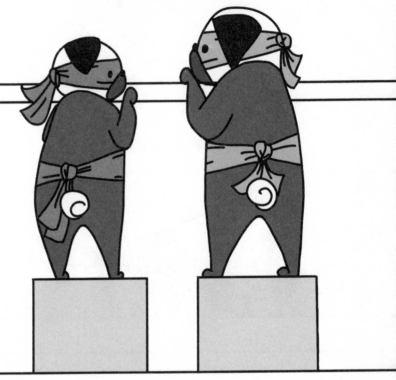

"What are they doing to him?" Rosy asked.

They watched as the pack of little humans ran around the classroom, shrieking with laughter as they tossed Mr. Bunny back and forth.

"I think they think he's a human toy. Not a dog toy."

"Ugh, that one just sneezed." Rosy pressed her face against the window, her breath fogging up the glass. "No, don't wipe your nose on him!"

Rosy turned frantically to Sunny. "We have to save him! What do we do?"

Sunny and Rosy tried many different ways to get into the building.

Locked!

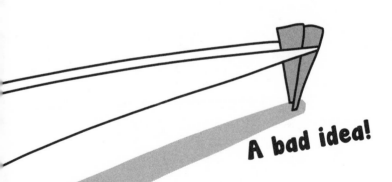

But they didn't have any success.

Sunny stood quietly as she thought about what Officer Bert would do. Finally, she pulled off her mask and said, "If we can't get in, we'll do a stakeout and wait until they come out. Then we'll rescue Mr. Bunny."

After they changed out of their ninja pug
suits, they stowed them in Sunny's backpack and hurled it over the fence. They
casually walked away, pretending to be
just two ordinary dogs wandering outside.

An hour later, a bell rang loudly from the big building. A second after that, the front doors flew open and a herd of little humans stormed out.

Sunny and Rosy searched the crowd in a panic for a few minutes before Rosy cried out.

Mr. Bunny was tucked into the pocket of a girl's backpack.

Sunny and Rosy watched his long ears bounce with each step the girl took as she ran to her mother. The girl skipped next to her mother as they disappeared around the corner.

Sunny gasped and Rosy squeaked in frustration.

"How are we going to follow them?" Rosy cried.

The wrinkle in Sunny's forehead deepened as she scanned the area for an idea.

With an excited snort, she jumped up and ran to grab something leaning against a trash can. "We'll keep up with them on these!"

CHAPTER 9

After a few turns, Sunny and Rosy ended up in front of a small blue house with a large porch and two bicycles in the front yard.

Leaving the skateboards on the curb,
Sunny and Rosy crouched behind a large
bush in front of the house.

"We're never going to get him back!"
Rosy groaned.

"Shh," Sunny said. "Look. Someone's
coming back out."

An older boy left the house and got on the larger of the two bicycles in the yard. The girl followed after him with Mr. Bunny in her arms.

Rosy's tail thumped against Sunny in her excitement at seeing Mr. Bunny again.

"Where are you going?" the girl asked. "Can I come too? It'll take just a second for me to get my helmet."

The older boy shook his head. "I'm going to hang out with my friends."

"Steve and Tyler? I can show them Ms. Bunny. It's such a weird story how I got her. They'll like it."

Rosy bounced as she huffed angrily, "Ms. Bunny? Ms. Bunny! Mr. Bunny is a he!"

Sunny shushed Rosy again.

"No," the older boy said. "You can't tag along. Go away and do whatever you want to do."

The little girl stared up at her brother and frowned. "But I don't want to do something by myself. I want to do something with you."

The older boy shrugged. "Sorry. No kid sisters."

The little girl stood for a long time in
the yard as she watched her brother
pedal away. "Fine," she said. "I don't need
to hang out with you and your friends.
I like being by myself." She clenched her
fists, and a high-pitched squeak brought
her attention down to the stuffy in her
hands. "That's right, Ms. Bunny. I'm not
alone. You're here."

The little girl put Mr. Bunny down on the front steps and ran into the house.

"Quick," cried out Rosy. "Now's our chance."
Before Sunny could stop her, Rosy was
racing toward the steps. But just as Rosy
reached out to grab Mr. Bunny, the door
creaked open.

With a squeak, Rosy hopped off the steps
and out of sight.

The little girl's arms were full of
stuffies, clean and carefully
mended and patched.

"Ms. Bunny, I'd like you to meet your new family. Welcome to your forever home!" After counting the toys in front of her, the little girl scrambled to her feet and shouted over her shoulder, "Oh, I forgot Mr. McFluffles. I'll be right back!"

As the little girl disappeared back inside,
Sunny crept forward and pulled Rosy
away. "It's time to go home."

"But what about Mr. Bunny?" asked Rosy.
"We haven't rescued him yet!"

"I think he's more
needed here,"
said Sunny.
"Don't you?"

Rosy watched the little girl return and introduce Mr. Bunny to her cluster of toys. Then Rosy looked up at Sunny.

"But you love Mr. Bunny," Rosy said. "Aren't you sad to leave him here?"

"Yes," said Sunny. "But I know he'll be happy here, and he'll be making some- one else happy."

Rosy stamped her paw and sighed. "I know she's happy, but I wanted to make you happy. I wanted to get him back for you."

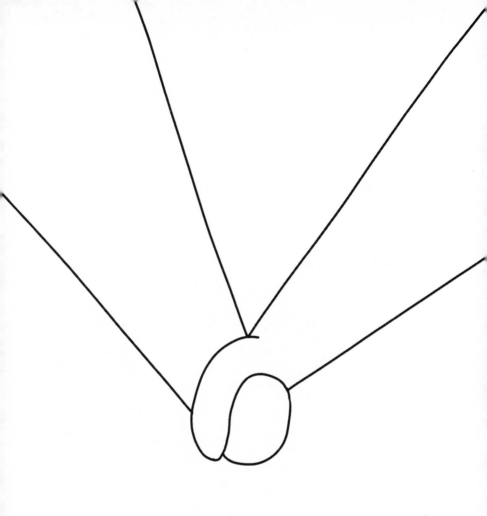

Sunny took Rosy's paw into her own.
"I am happy. I got you back."

Rosy stared at their intertwined paws.

And then, suddenly, she jumped up and attacked.

But instead of chewing on Sunny's drum-stick or slurping on her ears like before, Rosy hugged her sister tightly.

Sunny and Rosy trotted to the school to fetch Sunny's backpack and then back home just as the sun was beginning to set.

Even though they weren't returning home with Mr. Bunny, they knew Officer Bert would have been proud of the way they carried out their mission.

It just turned out it hadn't been a rescue mission after all. Instead, it had been a safety check on Mr. Bunny in his new forever home.

And both Sunny and Rosy
were okay with that.

Sunny and Rosy sighed as they closed the door behind them. It felt so good to be back home after a long day out.

First, they went into the kitchen and had a snack.

Then, once their bellies were full and all the crumbs had been licked up, they settled down for a nap.

By the time their human arrived, Sunny and Rosy were curled up together.

Their human carried a bag with ribbon straps. "I have presents," she said. She placed the bag in front of Sunny and Rosy. The paper wrapping inside the bag crinkled as they reached into it.

"A new toy for each of the two best dogs in the whole world!"

CHAPTER 10

Sunny and Rosy loved their Officer Bert stuffies almost as much as they loved each other.

Almost, but not quite.

Flora Ahn is an attorney by day, but by night, she's the author and illustrator of the cartoons on her blog, *Bah Humpug*. Although she tried to draw other things, her pugs, Sunny and Rosy, insistently barked and pawed at her until she made drawings of them. Lots and lots of drawings of them. She lives in Virginia, where she spies on her pugs and uses her observations to develop her blog and books.